The Dressing-Up Box

Written by Mairi Mackinnon

Illustrated by Kate Sheppard

How this book works

The story of **The Dressing-Up Box** has been written for you to read with your child. You take turns to read:

You read these words.

I'd like to be a mermaid.

I can sit on a rock.

4

Your child reads these words.

You don't have to finish the story in one session. If your child is getting tired, put a marker in the page and come back to it later.

You can find out more about helping your child with this book, and with reading in general, on pages 30-31.

The Dressing-Up Box

Turn the page to start the story.

I'd like to be a mermaid.

I can sit
on a rock.

Or maybe a circus acrobat –

I can get up
on top.

Perhaps I'll be
an artist.

I can pick
up a pen.

Or how about a
grizzly bear?

I can dig a den.

I'd like to sail the
seven seas.

I can mop
a deck.

Or watch me score
the winning goal –

I can kick
at a net.

I could be an explorer.

I can pack
a map.

Or maybe a sleeping princess.
Hush now!

I can nap.

Perhaps I'll be a superstar chef?

I can pick
up a pan.

I can be anything I like,

I can,

I can,

I can!

Puzzle 1

Match the speech bubbles to the pictures.

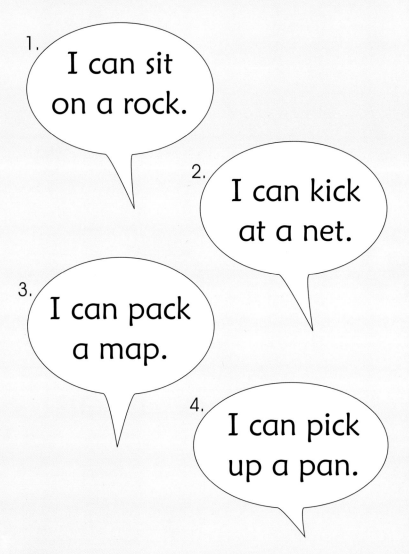

1. I can sit on a rock.

2. I can kick at a net.

3. I can pack a map.

4. I can pick up a pan.

Puzzle 2

Choose the right word to complete the sentence.

1.

I can get up on ....

mop	pop	top

2.

I can .... up a pen.

kick	lick	pick

3.

I can mop a ....

| deck | dock | duck |

4.

I can ....

| nag | nan | nap |

Puzzle 3

Look at the pictures, read the sentences, then say whether they are true or false.

1. **I am a cat.**

2. **I am sad.**

3. **I am sick.**

4. **I can kick.**

Answers to puzzles

Puzzle 1

1. I can sit on a rock. – D
2. I can kick at a net. – A
3. I can pack a map. – B
4. I can pick up a pan. – C

Puzzle 2

1. I can get up on <u>top</u>.
2. I can <u>pick</u> up a pen.
3. I can mop a <u>deck</u>.
4. I can <u>nap</u>.

Puzzle 3

1. True
2. False
3. False
4. True

Guidance notes

Usborne Very First Reading is a series of books, specially developed for children who are learning to read. In the early books in the series, you and your child take turns to read, and your child steadily builds the knowledge and confidence to read alone.

The words for your child to read in **The Dressing-Up Box** introduce these eight letters or letter-combinations:

(Note that in this story, **c**, **k** and **ck** all have the same sound.) These are often among the first letters that children learn to read at school. Later books in the series gradually introduce more letters, sounds and spelling patterns, while reinforcing the ones your child already knows.

You'll find lots more information about the structure of the series, advice on helping your child with reading, extra practice activities and games on the Very First Reading website,* **www.usborne.com/veryfirstreading**

*US readers go to **www.veryfirstreading.com**

Some questions and answers

- **Why do I need to read with my child?**
  Sharing stories and taking turns makes reading an enjoyable and fun activity for children. It also helps them to develop confidence and reading stamina, and to take part in an exciting story using very few words.

- **When is a good time to read?**
  Choose a time when you are both relaxed, but not too tired, and there are no distractions. Only read for as long as your child wants to — you can always try again another day.

- **What if my child gets stuck?**
  Don't simply read the problem word yourself, but prompt your child and try to find the right answer together. Similarly, if your child makes a mistake, go back and look at the word together. Don't forget to give plenty of praise and encouragement.

- **We've finished, now what do we do?**
  It's a good idea to read the story several times to give your child more practice and more confidence. Then you can try reading **Captain Mac** at the same level or, when your child is ready, go on to Book 3 in the series.

Edited by Jenny Tyler and Lesley Sims
Designed by Caroline Spatz

First published in 2010 by Usborne Publishing Ltd., Usborne House,
83-85 Saffron Hill, London EC1N 8RT, England. www.usborne.com
Copyright © 2010 Usborne Publishing Ltd.

USBORNE VERY FIRST READING

There are fifteen titles in the **Usborne Very First Reading** series, which has been specially developed to help children learn to read.

To find out more about the structure of the series, go to **www.veryfirstreading.com**